Sleepover Squad

#5 Pony Party!

Grab your pillow and join the

Sleepover Squad!

#1 *Sleeping Over*

#2 *Camping Out*

#3 *The Trouble with Brothers*

#4 *Keeping Secrets*

#5 *Pony Party!*

P. J. DENTON

Sleepover Squad

#5 Pony Party!

Illustrated by Julia Denos

ALADDIN PAPERBACKS

NEW YORK   LONDON   TORONTO   SYDNEY

ALADDIN PAPERBACKS

An imprint of Simon & Schuster Children's Publishing Division

1230 Avenue of the Americas, New York, NY 10020

Text copyright © 2008 by Catherine Hapka

Illustrations copyright © 2008 by Julia Denos

All rights reserved, including the right of reproduction in whole or in part in any form.

ALADDIN PAPERBACKS and related logo are registered trademarks of Simon & Schuster, Inc.

Designed by Karin Paprocki

The text of this book was set in Cochin.

Manufactured in the United States of America

First Aladdin Paperbacks edition June 2008

2 4 6 8 10 9 7 5 3 1

Library of Congress Control Number 2007937306

ISBN-13: 978-1-4169-5931-1

ISBN-10: 1-4169-5931-9

Sleepover Squad

#5 Pony Party!

1

A Very Special Secret

"Can't you drive any faster, Daddy?" Emily McDougal begged.

Her father was driving the family station wagon. He glanced back at Emily from the driver's seat.

"You wouldn't want me to get a speeding ticket, Emily-Memily," he said with a twinkle in his blue eyes. "If I did, it would take even longer to get to your friends' houses. We might even be late for the movie!"

Emily knew her father was right. Still, she couldn't help feeling impatient as he stopped at a stop sign. Another car crossed in front of them. It seemed to take forever to go by. Emily bit her lip and counted to five. Finally her father started driving again.

There were two reasons that Emily was so impatient. The first was that Mr. McDougal was taking Emily and her three best friends to the movies. They were going to see *The Unicorn Fairy*. The girls

had been dying to see that movie ever since they'd first heard about it.

But that wasn't the only reason Emily was excited. She had a secret—a big one! She couldn't wait to share it with her friends.

"Remember not to say anything about the big news, okay?" she reminded her father. "I want to wait until all four of us are together."

Mr. McDougal took one hand off the steering wheel just long enough to cross his heart. "Your secret is safe with me," he promised.

"Thanks, Daddy." Emily fiddled with the strap of her seat belt. Sometimes when she was feeling anxious or impatient or nervous, she tried to distract herself by wriggling her fingers or playing with her long, pale blond hair. But today it didn't work. She still felt her heart racing with excitement and her stomach flip-flopping eagerly.

She looked out the window. The McDougals lived out in the country, but their old farmhouse was only about a fifteen-minute drive from town. It was even closer to the subdivision at the edge of town where Emily's friend Jo Sanchez lived. They would be there soon. Emily just hoped she could wait that long!

Soon Emily's father was turning onto Larkspur Lane. Emily could see Jo standing out in front of the Sanchezes' tidy home. Jo was always right on time for everything. She waved when she saw the station wagon.

As soon as her father stopped, Emily reached over and opened the door. Jo climbed in beside her.

"Hi, Mr. McDougal," Jo said. "Thanks for taking me to the movies."

"You're very welcome." Mr. McDougal started the car up again.

Jo fastened her seat belt, then looked at Emily. "Hey, Emily, what's the matter with you?"

"What do you mean?" Emily tried to look and sound just like she always did. But it was no use. Her voice made a funny little squeak at the end. She giggled. "I'm just excited about the movie, that's all."

Jo wrinkled her nose. "Are you sure?" she asked. "You look funny."

Emily should have known. Jo always noticed things. That was part of what made her a good student. It also made her a good friend.

"Okay, you're right," Emily admitted. "I have a secret. But I can't tell you what it is yet."

"Why not?" Jo's brown eyes widened. "Does it have something to do with our sleepover at your house this Friday night?"

"Maybe." Emily smiled. "But that's all I'm going to say about it until we pick up Taylor and Kara!"

It wasn't easy, but she stuck to her word. Jo was pretty patient. She didn't try to make Emily say anything else.

A few minutes later they reached town and pulled to the curb in front of a brick house with faded black shutters and a big front porch. A red-haired teenage boy was mowing the patch of grass between the porch and the sidewalk. He saw them and turned off the mower.

"Kaaaaaraaaaa!" he yelled at the house. "Your ride's here!"

Emily waved at the boy through the open car window. "Hi, Chip!" she called. Chip was the oldest of Kara Wyatt's four brothers. He waved back, then started the mower again.

A moment later Kara burst out of the house and ran toward the car, her wavy red hair bouncing everywhere. She opened the door and jumped into the third row of seats.

"Hi, guys," she cried breathlessly. "Guess what? My mom gave me extra money for snacks. I think I have enough to get popcorn *and* candy!"

"Guess what else?" Jo said. "Emily has a secret about our sleepover. But she won't tell me what it is."

Mr. McDougal was looking at the girls in the rearview mirror. "Seat belt please, Kara," he said as he started the car again.

"Oops! I almost forgot." Kara giggled and clicked on her seat belt. "So what's the big secret? Come on, Em, you have to tell us!"

"Sorry," Emily said with a grin. She already knew that Kara wasn't very good at waiting. "I don't want to say anything until the whole Sleepover Squad is together."

Emily, Jo, and Kara, along with Taylor Kent, were all members of the Sleepover Squad. They'd named themselves that while planning their very first sleepover at Taylor's house. Since then, they'd all taken turns hosting other sleepovers. This weekend it was Emily's turn again.

"Please please please!" Kara cried. "You have to tell us now, or I might die! Come on, Em—we won't let Taylor know you told us first! *Pleeeeeease?*"

It seemed to take forever to drive the four blocks between Kara's house and Taylor's. After a while both Emily and Jo covered their ears to block out Kara's begging. In the front seat, Mr. McDougal turned on the radio.

But finally the car stopped in front of the Kents' big stone house, which was right in the middle of one of the nicest blocks in town. Taylor was kicking a soccer ball against the trunk of one of the big trees along the sidewalk. When she saw the station wagon, she kicked the ball toward the house and jogged over.

"Hurry up!" Kara cried as soon as Taylor opened the car door. "Emily is keeping us in suspense."

"Huh?" Taylor had to duck to climb into the seat beside Kara. She was taller than any of her friends. "What's she talking about, Emmers?"

Emily took a deep breath. Finally everyone was here. It was time to share her secret.

She glanced forward at her father. He winked at her in the rearview mirror and then started the car.

"Next stop, *The Unicorn Fairy*!" he said.

Kara leaned forward and poked Emily in the shoulder. "Come on!" she whined. "You said you'd tell us your secret when Taylor was here!"

Emily nodded and looked around. Three sets of curious eyes stared back at her. Taylor's greenish-gold ones looked kind of confused.

"What's all this about a secret?" Taylor asked. "Is it about the movie?"

"No, it has something to do with the sleepover," Jo told her. "That's all I know."

Kara bounced up and down in her seat. "Tell us, tell us, tell us!" she chanted impatiently.

Emily giggled. "I will, if you'll all be quiet for a second." She took another deep breath. "Here it is: My mom's friend Ms. Sullivan is going to bring a real live pony to our sleepover!"

2

Pony Plans

"No way!" Kara shrieked. "A pony? For real?"

Jo clapped her hands. "Wow! I can't believe it!"

"I can," Taylor said with a grin. "If anybody could figure out how to get a pony to our sleepover, it's Emmers!"

They all laughed at that, including Emily. Everyone knew that Emily loved horses and ponies. She had tons of books about horses on the bookshelf in her room at home. She also had two shelves filled with model horses. Her dream was to take riding lessons someday, although her parents always said she was still too young for that.

"What's the pony's name?" Jo asked.

"What does it look like?" Kara cried. "Will we get to ride it?"

"The pony's name is Ladybug," Emily said. She tried to remember everything her mother had told her about Ladybug. "I'm not sure what she looks like, though. I've

never seen her. But Ms. Sullivan is planning to bring her over on Saturday morning. She's going to let us help brush Ladybug and tack her up—that means put on her saddle and bridle. Then she'll give each of us a mini riding lesson."

She shivered as she said the last part. Her mother had explained that the "lessons" would be very short and simple. Ms. Sullivan would teach the girls just enough to ride Ladybug around the yard safely. Still, even that was a lot closer to a *real* lesson than the pony rides at the fair! Emily had dreamed about taking riding lessons for so long that she could hardly believe it was finally going to happen— at least for one day.

"This is going to be awesome," Taylor said, rubbing her short, curly dark hair with one hand. "I wonder if it will be like that trail ride I went on during my family's vacation out west."

"My grandpapa used to ride when he was a kid in Mexico," Jo said. "He tells crazy stories all the time about riding the range and roping bucking broncos and stuff like that."

Kara still looked excited. But now she looked a little nervous, too. "I hope Ladybug's not *too* big," she said. "Or too fast, either. I liked that short, fat, spotted pony they had at the fair last time. He was only a little bigger than Chester." Chester was the Wyatts' Labrador retriever. "He was almost as lazy as Chester too!"

"Don't worry," Taylor told Kara. "If Ladybug turns out to be too big and fast for you, I'll take your turn riding."

"No way!" Kara said quickly.

"Did you guys know that ponies are measured in hands?" Emily said. "One hand equals four inches."

"That's cool." Taylor held up her hands and spread out her long, slim fingers. "And

I'll tell you what else. I can't wait to get my *hands* on that pony!"

That made everyone laugh. But Emily was still thinking about some of the facts she'd learned from her horse books.

"That's how you tell a horse from a pony," she told her friends. "By how many hands tall it is."

"I wonder what color Ladybug is?" Kara giggled. "I wonder if she's red— you know, like a real ladybug."

"A red pony would be called a chestnut," Emily put in. She wondered if anyone had heard what she'd said about the difference between ponies and horses. It didn't seem like it.

"Or maybe she's spotted," Jo said. "Ladybugs have spots, too, remember?"

"Ooh, good one!" Kara exclaimed. "I bet you're right, Jo!"

Emily thought about telling her friends that a spotted horse or pony was called a pinto. But she decided not to bother—her friends were too excited to pay attention to her information right now. That was okay, though. Today was only Wednesday. That left plenty of time to teach them some of the stuff she knew about ponies before Saturday morning when Ladybug arrived.

"This is going to be the best sleepover ever," she said with a happy sigh.

"Wow, that was the best movie I ever saw in my whole life!" Kara exclaimed as the four girls walked out of the movie theater a couple of hours later.

Mr. McDougal was sitting on a bench in the theater lobby reading a book. He stood up when he saw them.

"How was the film, girls?" he asked.

"Awesome!" Taylor said.

Emily nodded. "The unicorn was so beautiful," she said. "I loved her silvery-white mane and tail."

"The coolest part was when she did that funny dance," Jo put in. "Remember?"

Kara giggled. "I wonder if Ladybug will dance like that for us?"

"Actually, horses can't move like the unicorn did in the dance," Emily began. "See, when they trot, they—"

"Oh, okay," Kara said before she could finish, not sounding very interested. She waved her almost empty popcorn box. "Anyway, how about the part when they jumped over that river?"

"Oh, yeah!" Taylor's eyes lit up. "Wasn't that cool?"

Emily bit her lip, feeling a tiny twinge of frustration as her friends chattered on about the movie. Didn't they want to learn more about ponies before the big day?

"Come on, girls," Mr. McDougal said. "I'd better get you home before your parents think you all ran away to join the circus."

Kara shook her head. "No way!" she said. "If we joined the circus, we'd miss our chance to ride at the pony sleepover this weekend."

"True. But they have lots of horses in the circus," Jo pointed out with her usual logic. "So we could still ride."

Emily laughed along with the others as they walked out of the theater into the hot late-afternoon sunshine. She knew she shouldn't feel so annoyed with her friends for not paying attention to everything she said. They were still excited about the party, that was all.

3

Antici-pony-pation!

"Happy Friday morning, everyone!" Emily sang out when she danced into the kitchen. Her parents were already there. Her father was eating breakfast and reading the newspaper. He was still wearing his pajamas and bathrobe. He was a high school teacher, so he had the summer off just like Emily did.

Emily's mother was sorting a big pile of beans at the counter. She ran an organic nursery out of their home and grew all sorts of fruits and vegetables. That kept her busy all spring and summer long. But in the winter, she had more time to take care of Emily and the house while Mr. McDougal was at work. Emily thought her parents made a perfect team.

"Good morning, Emily," Mrs. McDougal said, glancing over her shoulder. "You're certainly full of energy today."

"I guess." Emily danced over to the cabinet and took out a glass. "Hey, Mom, did you check the carrot patch yet? I want to make sure we'll have enough for the pony."

Her father looked up from the newspaper and smiled. "Ponies, ponies, ponies," he teased. "It seems like that's all you talk about anymore, Emily-Memily."

Emily giggled. She knew he was just joking around. Both her parents had spent the past two days helping her come up with ideas to turn that night's sleepover into

a pony-themed party. The rest of the Sleepover Squad was coming over right after lunch. As part of the sleepover, they were going to help finish decorating and setting up for Ladybug's arrival the next morning. There was a lot to do when a pony was invited to your party!

"Sorry," she said with a smile. "I guess I'm just looking forward to this sleepover. Even more than usual, I mean."

"I know the perfect word for that." Her father looked over at her mother and raised one eyebrow playfully. "I think we could call it . . . antici-pony-pation."

Mrs. McDougal groaned. "Oh, dear," she said. "That's a terrible joke, Arthur." She tossed a bean at him. "But don't worry, Emily. I'm sure I can dig up some carrots for our visitor." She winked. "Get it? Dig up?"

Mr. McDougal groaned. "Terrible pun, Felicity!" he told Emily's mom. "But I might forgive you if you bring me another cup of tea. . . ."

Emily was so excited that she could hardly sit still long enough to eat her breakfast. She finished quickly, then helped clear the table.

When she checked the clock, she saw that she still had more than three hours to wait before her friends were supposed to arrive. Was there anything else she needed to do to get ready for the pony party?

She wasn't sure, so she decided to check her books for more ideas.

She went up to her room and looked at her bookshelf. Spotting her favorite horse-care book, she pulled it out. Next to it she saw a big book about horse breeds. It had tons of great photos of ponies and horses. She couldn't resist pulling that one out too.

I can't wait to meet Ladybug tomorrow, she thought as she paged through the photo book. *This is going to be the most perfect sleepover ever.*

She turned another page. The next section was about a breed of horse called the Arabian. The photo showed a gleaming white horse with big, dark eyes and a silky mane and tail. It looked a little bit like the unicorn from the movie she'd seen with her friends.

Emily stared at the photo, picturing what it would be like to care for and ride the pretty Arabian in the photo just as the fairy had done with the unicorn in the movie. Then she shivered as she realized that the very next day she would get to help groom and ride a real, live pony.

She closed her eyes to help her imagine it better. In her imagination she could see herself patting a pony. She didn't know what Ladybug looked like, so she pictured her looking a little bit like the pretty white horse in her book, only shorter.

Maybe Ladybug would have a silky white mane that she could help brush. She could even see it sparkle a little, just like the unicorn's silvery mane and tail. Emily would brush it until it glistened. Then she would give the pony a carrot as a treat, and the pony would nuzzle her to say thank you.

After that they would walk together to the edge of a grassy field like the one behind her house. Emily would leap onto Ladybug's back, and they would canter off together across the field.

Emily sighed happily. She could imagine it so clearly! In fact, she could almost feel Ladybug's silky mane on her hands. . . .

"Hey!" she blurted out. Her eyes flew open as she felt something soft against her arm. Then she laughed as she saw that it was her cat. "Mi-Mo! I didn't know you were in here."

The cat started purring, then rubbed against her again. Emily grabbed him and hugged him. His long whiskers tickled her chin.

"Oh, Mi-Mo," she whispered in his furry ear. "Tomorrow is going to be the best day of my life!"

4

Horsing Around

"Emily! Your friends are here!" Mrs. McDougal called a few hours later.

Emily looked up from her horse-care book. After daydreaming about riding Ladybug for a while, she'd gone downstairs to help her parents finish preparing for the sleepover. Then, after lunch, she'd gone back upstairs to look for more ideas in her books.

"Coming, Mom!" she called back.

She closed the book and set it on the shelf. Mi-Mo was sleeping on her bed, and she gave him a pat. Then she headed for the door.

Taylor, Kara, and Jo were waiting for her in the keeping room. That was what Emily's parents called the big room beside the kitchen. It had a huge stone fireplace, beams on the ceiling, and a creaky wooden floor covered with rag rugs. There was a big, squishy couch facing the fireplace and a cabinet full of games and puzzles. Emily and her friends loved hanging out in there. It was always toasty warm in the winter and nice and cool in the summer. They were planning to sleep there that night instead of up in Emily's room, which could be stuffy in the summer. Emily's friends had already piled their backpacks and sleeping bags in the corner.

"Giddyup, Emmers!" Taylor exclaimed

when Emily came in. "We're ready to get this pony party started."

Kara giggled. "She's been talking like that the whole way over here," she said, pointing at Taylor.

Taylor shrugged. "I'm just getting in the pony spirit, that's all." She poked Emily in the shoulder. "Hey, that reminds me, I had a great idea. Why don't we see if Ladybug's owner will let us play Pony Express while she's here tomorrow? We learned about that in school, remember? We can gallop around and pretend to deliver the mail."

"Um, I don't know if that's such a good idea," Emily said. "None of us really know how to ride. We probably won't be able to gallop after one lesson."

"What do you mean?" Kara shrugged. "We've all ridden tons of times at the fair. It's easy."

"Riding at the fair is different," Emily explained. "There's always someone leading those ponies. When we ride Ladybug—"

"Hey!" Jo interrupted. She had just walked over to look at the pile of stuffed horses Emily had brought down from her room as decorations for the party. Bending down, Jo grabbed the biggest one. It was white with a pink mane and tail. "I never noticed this one before. It's really cute—it looks kind of like the unicorn from the movie."

"Really? Let me see." Taylor hurried over and grabbed the stuffed horse. She tucked it between her legs, pretending to ride around the room on it. "Nope! It's not a unicorn," she said with a grin. "See? It's not flying."

"Hey, Em, what are we having to eat at this sleepover?" Kara licked her lips. She was always very interested in food, because she was almost always hungry. "I was hoping we could have some cheese puffs as a snack for us and Ladybug. See,

I know ponies love carrots, so they probably like cheese puffs, too."

Jo blinked at her. "Huh? Why?"

"Duh. They're both orange!" Kara said.

Emily bit her lip. She couldn't help thinking that some of her friends' ideas about ponies were a little silly.

"Um, I don't think ponies are supposed to eat cheese puffs," she told Kara. Then she glanced around at the others. "They mostly eat grass and hay, and some also eat grain. For snacks, they like carrots and apples and things like that."

Taylor was still pretending to ride around on the pink-and-white stuffed horse. She jogged over to the magazine basket near the couch and jumped over it.

"Check it out, this pony can jump," she said. "I wonder if Ladybug can jump over walls and stuff like the horses I've seen in the Olympics."

Kara's eyes widened. "Or like that unicorn in the movie!" she said. "It jumped over a whole river, remember? I heard horses are really good at jumping over stuff."

"Maybe we can ride Ladybug down into the woods behind the house and see if she'll jump over the stream," Taylor suggested. "What do you think, Emmers?"

"I'm not sure Ms. Sullivan would like that," Emily said. "It will probably be tiring enough for Ladybug just having us all ride her. But don't worry, we'll still have lots of fun. Anyway, I have lots of ideas for other games we can play this afternoon. My dad said he'd set up a game of horseshoes for us in the backyard and teach us how to play."

"If horses wear shoes, why don't they wear socks?" Kara joked.

Jo pointed to Kara's feet. Kara was wearing a pair of flip-flops. "Why should they?" Jo said. "People don't always wear socks either."

"Who cares?" Taylor sounded a little impatient. "All I know is, I can't wait to try riding the range!" She ran over to the couch and jumped onto one of the arms, sitting on it as if it were a horse. "Giddyup, Ladybug!" she cried, kicking at the couch. "You have to run faster than that if we're going to win the Kentucky Derby!"

Just then Mi-Mo wandered into the room. He was heading toward the mud-room, where his food bowl was. But he stopped and stared at Taylor riding the couch, his whiskers twitching.

"Run, Mi-Mo!" Kara cried with a laugh. "Otherwise Taylor will probably try to ride you next!"

Taylor laughed and threw the stuffed horse at her. Jo laughed too.

But Emily just sighed. The sleepover had officially started, and her friends still seemed a lot more interested in goofing around than they were in learning more about ponies.

Still, she reminded herself that that made sense. To her friends, a pony party was just a fun new way to have a sleepover. They didn't care as much as she did about learning every detail involving ponies and riding. And that was okay. She would be the same way if, for example, Taylor decided to have a soccer-themed sleepover.

But she couldn't help wishing they would take things just a *little* more seriously. . . .

That night Emily was tired. But she couldn't fall asleep. She stared up at the shadowy ceiling of the keeping room, thinking about how her friends had been acting. The sleepover had been fun so far, as usual. The girls had played horseshoes, helped Emily's father make horse-shaped cookies, and watched a horse DVD.

But even with all the horse-themed stuff at the sleepover, Emily's friends still didn't seem to care that they didn't know anything about ponies. It was bad enough that they didn't want to listen to Emily when she tried to teach them. But what if they didn't listen to Ms. Sullivan tomorrow morning, either? What if they ended up accidentally hurting Ladybug because they didn't know enough? What if they fell off when they tried to ride because they didn't pay attention?

All the "what if" questions kept swirling around her brain, making it impossible to sleep. Finally Emily sat up so fast that she startled Mi-Mo. He had been curled up at the foot of her sleeping bag, but now he meowed and jumped up on the sofa.

"Sorry, Mi-Mo," Emily whispered.

She pushed back the covers and climbed out of her sleeping bag, being very careful not to wake up her friends. All three of them were sound asleep. Taylor was sprawled out on her stomach. Her sleeping bag was pushed halfway down her legs, and she was using one of Emily's stuffed horses as a pillow. Jo was curled up in a little ball with her sleeping bag pulled up to her chin. Kara was lying on her back, snoring softly.

Emily tiptoed past them, then headed for the stairs. She was careful to skip the creaky one near the bottom. There was a full moon, so her room was almost as bright with moonlight as it was in the daytime. She went over to her bookcase and peered at her horse books. Reading in bed always helped her fall asleep. She chose one of her favorite books, a chapter book called *Beach Pony*. She also grabbed a tiny flashlight from her bedside table. Then she tiptoed back downstairs and slipped into her sleeping bag again.

Sure enough, she had only read one chapter when her eyes started to feel heavy. Turning off the flashlight and dropping the book on the pillow beside her, she snuggled into her sleeping bag.

This time she didn't think about her friends at all. The only thing in her head as she fell asleep was the image of herself cantering Ladybug along a beautiful, sandy beach.

5

Meeting Ladybug

By the next morning, Emily had all but forgotten her worries about her friends. She was too excited about the pony's arrival to think about anything else. Ms. Sullivan and Ladybug were supposed to arrive at nine thirty, but Emily and her friends were waiting out on the front lawn of Emily's house by nine fifteen.

"Here she comes!" Kara shrieked a few minutes later. She jumped up and down and clapped her hands. "Finally! I see the horse trailer!"

"Don't you mean pony trailer?" Taylor glanced up from tying her shoe. She was wearing a pair of Mrs. McDougal's hiking boots. That was because she'd forgotten she wasn't supposed to wear sneakers or sandals to ride, even though Emily had told her at least three times in the past few days. Luckily Taylor had big feet for her age, and Mrs. McDougal had small ones. The boots were a little bit big, but they were close enough.

"Stand back, girls," Mr. McDougal said as the truck and trailer came closer.

Emily held her breath. She couldn't wait to see Ladybug!

"Hello, hello!" The woman driving the truck waved at the girls through the open window. Then she eased to a stop in the shade of several big maple trees and climbed out. She was a cheerful-looking woman with messy hair that was mostly brown with a few streaks of gray. Her eyes crinkled at the corners when she smiled, and she was very tan.

"Girls, this is Ms. Sullivan," Mrs. McDougal said. "And these are the girls." She introduced them each by name.

"Nice to meet you, girls." Ms. Sullivan

rubbed her hands together. "Are you ready to meet Ladybug?"

All four of the girls cheered. "We've been waiting all week for this!" Kara added excitedly.

"All right. I'll get her out in a second." Ms. Sullivan smiled at them. "First, I just want to talk to you a little bit about how to be safe around ponies."

See? Emily thought. *If my friends had listened to me, they would already know all about that!*

But she didn't say it out loud. She listened as Ms. Sullivan explained that they shouldn't run or scream or make sudden movements when they were close to the pony.

"Ladybug is pretty calm as ponies go," Ms. Sullivan finished. "But better safe than sorry—that's my motto!"

"And a fine motto it is," Mr. McDougal put in with a chuckle.

Taylor was staring at the trailer. "Can she come out now?"

"Yes, I think it's time. Come this way, girls." Ms. Sullivan led the way to the back of her trailer. She told them to stand off to one side a little. Then she swung open the big metal doors at the back of the trailer and stepped inside.

Emily held her breath. She heard a clang from inside, then a snort. A moment later Ms. Sullivan reappeared. Beside her, peering out curiously, was the cutest pony Emily had ever seen.

"Oh my gosh!" Jo exclaimed softly. "She's so cute!"

Ladybug was short and stout, with a sweet face and long eyelashes. Her shiny coat was white with reddish-brown spots. She stepped down carefully from the trailer and followed Ms. Sullivan as she led her over to the wide, flat, grassy part of the yard between the maple trees and the raspberry patch.

"All right, you can come say hi now," Ms. Sullivan called.

"Gently, girls!" Mrs. McDougal reminded them.

Up until then Emily had still been a little worried about how her friends would act around the pony. But she forgot all about that now. All she could think about was how adorable Ladybug was.

"Hey, girl," she said softly as she stepped closer. She carefully reached out and stroked Ladybug's velvety nose. She giggled as the pony breathed out, warming Emily's hand with her breath. "She's a mare, right?" Emily asked Ms. Sullivan.

"That's right, Emily." Ms. Sullivan glanced around at the others, who had also stepped forward to pat the pony. "A mare is what we call a female horse like Ladybug. Now, would you all like to brush her?"

"Yeah!" Kara started to cheer loudly. Then she remembered she wasn't supposed to be loud around the pony. She clapped one hand over her mouth. "Oops," she said through her hand. "Sorry, Ladybug!"

The three adults laughed at that. "It's okay, Kara," Mr. McDougal teased. "We know keeping you quiet is a lost cause!"

All the girls giggled, including Kara. "I'm trying!" she insisted.

Ms. Sullivan took a bucket out of her truck. It was full of brushes and rubber currycombs. "Here's how you do it," she said, demonstrating as she talked. "The currycomb loosens the dust and dirt from Ladybug's coat. Rub it in a circular motion, like this. Then you can use the brush to brush the dirt away."

She handed each girl a currycomb and a brush, then told them to go to work. Emily picked a spot at Ladybug's shoulder. As she slowly curried and brushed the pony's soft coat, she watched her friends.

Jo was very precise. She would rub the currycomb in one circle, then carefully brush away every bit of dust she'd raised.

Taylor was easily distracted. Sometimes she would use the currycomb and then forget to use the brush. Or she would just use the brush without the curry. Or she would notice a fly buzzing around and chase it off, forgetting all about grooming.

Then there was Kara. She brushed Ladybug a few times, but then she started playing with her shaggy mane. Soon she'd dropped her tools entirely and was running her hands through Ladybug's mane.

"Can I braid her mane?" she asked. "She'd look really cute that way!"

Emily bit her lip. She wished her friends had listened to her more this week. If they had, they might know more about ponies now.

"Don't be silly," she told Kara with a little frown. "Ponies don't like their manes braided."

Kara looked surprised. "Oh," she said. "Sorry."

"No, don't be sorry, dear," Ms. Sullivan said. "Actually, it's quite common to braid a pony's mane. Ladybug gets hers braided whenever she's in a show."

Emily felt stupid. "Oh," she said softly. "I guess I never read about that in any of my horse books."

Ms. Sullivan smiled at her. "Don't fret, Emily," she said. "Just keep reading and you'll keep learning. After all, nobody knows everything there is to know about ponies."

"Not even you?" Taylor asked.

Ms. Sullivan laughed. So did Emily's parents.

"Nope," Ms. Sullivan told Taylor with a smile that made her eyes crinkle even more. "Not even me."

That made Emily feel better. So what if she didn't know *everything* about ponies? The important thing was, she was crazy about Ladybug. She couldn't wait to ride her!

6

Riding High

"**O**kay, girls," Ms. Sullivan said a few minutes later. "Ladybug looks good. I think it's time to ride."

"Cool!" Taylor cried, tossing her brush aside. "Let's go!"

Ms. Sullivan handed Emily the lead line attached to Ladybug's halter. "Here, Emily," she said. "Why don't you hold her while I get the tack?"

"Okay." Emily held on to the rope with

both hands. She gazed at Ladybug, wondering what it was going to be like to ride her. For a second she felt nervous.

She forgot about that when Ms. Sullivan returned from the truck carrying a saddle. A bridle was hanging over her shoulder.

"Here you go, Kara," Ms. Sullivan said, handing over the bridle. "Hold this while we get the saddle on."

Kara grabbed the bridle with both hands. It was made of leather straps with a few bits of metal. She held it up and stared at it.

"What's that metal part for?" she asked.

"That's called the bit," Emily spoke up before Ms. Sullivan could answer. "It goes in the pony's mouth."

"That's right," Ms. Sullivan said. She was spreading a pad on Ladybug's back. Then she set the saddle on the pad.

"Ew. Really?" Kara wrinkled her nose

and held the bridle a little farther away. She didn't like to get dirty.

"Take a look at what I'm doing, girls," Ms. Sullivan said. She explained how to position the pad and saddle and then do up the strap that held it in place.

"That's called a girth, right?" Emily said eagerly, pointing at the strap.

Ms. Sullivan smiled at her. "It would be if this were an English saddle," she said. "But since it's a Western saddle, we call it the cinch."

Taylor laughed. "Hey!" she said. "Tacking up this pony is a cinch! Get it?"

Everyone laughed. Emily was a little distracted, though. She couldn't believe how much she still didn't know about ponies!

But she brightened up as Ms. Sullivan finished tightening the cinch and then put on Ladybug's bridle. It was almost time to ride!

Ms. Sullivan had brought a riding helmet for the girls to borrow. She sent Mr. McDougal to the truck to fetch it.

"Okay," she said, looking around at the girls. "Who's first?"

Taylor, Jo, and Kara all looked at Emily. "Emmers can go first," Taylor said.

"Really?" Emily smiled at her friends. She knew they were all eager to ride too. It was nice of them to let her go first. "Thanks, guys!"

The riding helmet was made of black plastic. It was sort of like Emily's bike helmet, only it came down a little farther on her head. Ms. Sullivan helped Emily put it on. Then she led Ladybug over to a big stump near the maple trees.

"All right, Emily," she said. "We can use this stump as a mounting block. That will make it easier to get on. Climb up on the stump and grab a hunk of Ladybug's mane—don't worry, it won't hurt her.

Then put your left foot in the stirrup and swing your other leg over."

"Okay." Emily climbed onto the stump. Then she took a deep breath and grabbed a handful of the pony's mane. She hoped that Ms. Sullivan was right about it not hurting her. Emily hated it when anyone pulled her own hair. She tried to hold the mane gently just in case. Then she stuck her foot in the stirrup.

"Hang on," Ms. Sullivan said right away. "Other foot!"

"Oops!" Emily blushed. She'd accidentally put her right foot into the stirrup instead of her left. If she tried to get on that way, she'd end up sitting on Ladybug facing backward!

She wished everyone wasn't watching her. It made her a little nervous. But she tried to forget about that as she put her left foot in the stirrup.

This time she did everything right.

Seconds later she was sitting in the saddle. It felt great!

"Good job," Ms. Sullivan said as she helped Emily put her right foot in the right stirrup.

"You look terrific up there, Em!" Mr. McDougal called.

"Thanks." Emily smiled. She could hardly believe it. She was riding!

"Okay, pick up the reins." Ms. Sullivan showed her how. It was a little tricky, but Emily had practiced using the pictures in her books and an old jump rope. So she got it right on the first try.

"Is it fun so far, Em?" Kara called.

"Uh-huh." Emily didn't look over at her friends. She was too busy making sure she kept holding the reins correctly.

"When we start moving, you'll want to keep your heels down. Like this, see?" Ms. Sullivan grabbed Emily's foot and pulled on it so that her toe in the stirrup

was pointing up and her heel was down.

"Okay, I knew that," Emily said, remembering her books. She tried to get her other foot to match the one Ms. Sullivan had fixed.

"Hold on to your reins," Ms. Sullivan instructed.

"Oops!" Emily looked down. The reins had slipped out of her hands while she was focusing on her feet. She gathered them up again. "Okay, I'm ready."

"Hi-ho, Ladybug!" Taylor called, laughing. "You're ready to gallop off into the sunset now!"

Jo looked at her watch. "Sunset? It's not even lunchtime yet!"

"No galloping for now," Ms. Sullivan said with a chuckle. "We'll start with a walk. Ready, Emily?"

Emily nodded. She didn't dare say anything—she was afraid that if she did, she would forget about her reins or her heels! So far this was much harder than she remembered from those pony rides.

Ms. Sullivan led Ladybug forward at a slow walk. Emily tried to hold her hands in place. She tried to keep both her heels down. There was a lot to remember! But she did her best to follow all the instructions Ms. Sullivan gave her. They walked all the way around the flat part of the yard twice.

"You're doing great, Emily," Ms. Sullivan said. "Want to try a little trot now?"

Emily's stomach flip-flopped. The ponies at the fair weren't allowed to go faster than a walk, which meant she had never trotted before. She glanced over at her friends. All three of them looked excited.

"Okay," she replied before she could lose her nerve. "That sounds fun."

"Ready? Here we go." Ms. Sullivan clucked to Ladybug. Then she jogged off. The pony started walking, but then broke into a jog herself. It felt much bouncier than her walk.

"Whoa!" Emily exclaimed in surprise as she felt herself sway.

Ladybug stopped suddenly. Emily tipped forward. She had to drop the reins and catch herself with the horn at the front of the saddle.

"Sorry about that, Emily," Ms. Sullivan told her. "I forgot to warn you that Ladybug speaks English. Whenever someone says, 'Whoa,' she stops."

"Oh. Okay." Emily felt her cheeks turning pink. "Sorry. I didn't mean to make her stop. I was just surprised. It felt so different."

"Yes, it does. But you did fine for your first time." Ms. Sullivan smiled up at her. "Want to try walking on your own before your friends have a turn?"

"Sure," Emily said. "What do I do?"

"Just hold on to the reins like you've been doing," Ms. Sullivan said. "Give her a little kick and say, 'Walk.' You can pull gently on the left rein if you want to turn

left, and the right one to go right. Not too hard, though—ponies have sensitive mouths! If you want her to stop—"

"Just say, 'Whoa'?" Emily guessed.

The woman smiled. "You got it!"

She let go of Ladybug's head. Emily took a deep breath. The ponies at the fair weren't allowed to go without someone leading them. Now Emily would finally know how it felt to ride for real!

"Here we go, Ladybug," she whispered. "Walk!"

The pony just stood there. "Don't forget to kick!" Jo called helpfully.

Emily had forgotten about that. She nudged at Ladybug with her heel. "Walk, Ladybug," she said a little louder. "Please?"

Finally the pony took a few steps forward. Emily smiled. She was riding!

After a few more steps Ladybug started turning too far to the left. Emily pulled as gently as she could on the right rein, but Ladybug kept drifting left. A second later she suddenly lowered her head. Emily was still holding on to the reins, and she wasn't expecting the pony to do that. The motion jerked her forward in the saddle. She ended up with the horn poking her in the stomach and her face in Ladybug's mane!

7

Taking Turns

"**O**ops!" Emily scrambled to push herself upright again, feeling embarrassed. "Did I mess up?"

Ms. Sullivan chuckled. "No, you did fine. Ladybug is always hungry, that's all. She decided it was time to eat grass." She walked over and made Ladybug lift her head up again. "Good job for your first solo ride, Emily. Want to let your friends try now?"

Emily wished she could ride longer. She was sure that if she practiced more, she would get better at it. It was harder than she'd expected! But she knew her friends were eager to have their turn, so she nodded.

Her father hurried over and helped her jump down from the saddle. "Okay, who's next?" he asked.

"We already drew straws." Taylor held up a twig. "I won."

Kara smacked her on the shoulder and giggled. "You did not!" she cried. "I did!"

"Kara's right," Jo spoke up. "She gets to go next."

Emily smiled as the grown-ups laughed. She wished her friends wouldn't goof around so much at a time like this. But she figured asking Taylor and Kara not to fool around would be like asking the sun not to shine. Or like asking a hungry pony not to eat grass.

Kara was still giggling as she climbed up on the stump. "Which foot do I want again?" she asked, lifting one foot and then the other and staring at them.

"Left foot in the stirrup," Ms. Sullivan said.

Kara stuck her left foot into the stirrup. Ladybug shifted her weight, and Kara yelped and pulled her foot back.

"What's she doing?" she exclaimed. "Wait, let me try again."

It took a few tries, but finally Kara was in the saddle. She did her best to pick up the reins, but they kept getting tangled in her fingers. "Can't I just hold on to the horn thingy?" she asked Ms. Sullivan. "I think I might need a handle, anyway."

"All right. Heels down, Kara." Ms. Sullivan led Ladybug around the yard again. Kara clung to the horn, leaning forward and giggling loudly with every step. Emily noticed that after a few seconds her friend's heels started pointing up instead of down, but she didn't say anything.

"Good job, Kara!" Emily called as her father helped Kara slide down a few minutes later. She felt a teensy bit relieved. Kara had had even more trouble than she had.

See? she told herself. *Riding is hard! I did fine for my first time, just like Ms. Sullivan said.*

Taylor was already stepping forward. "Okay, this time it really *is* my turn," she said, hopping up on the stump.

Taylor didn't have to ask which foot to use. She stuck her left foot in the stirrup and swung up into the saddle as if she'd done it a million times.

"Okay, how do I hold these things again?" she asked, picking up the reins. "Like this?"

"Almost." Ms. Sullivan adjusted Taylor's grip. "Like that. Got it?"

"Uh-huh." Taylor sat up straight and smiled. "This is fun! Let's go!"

Ms. Sullivan reached for her foot. "In a second," she said. "First, let's get your heels down."

"Oh, right." Taylor adjusted her feet before Ms. Sullivan could do it. "I heard you tell Emmers that. Okay, got it!"

Ms. Sullivan had to correct Taylor only a few times as they walked around. When it was time to trot, they went all the way around the yard. Taylor didn't lose her balance at all.

"Wow, that was fun!" Taylor exclaimed when they stopped. "Do I get to ride by myself now like Emmers did?"

"Sure, give it a try." Ms. Sullivan let go of Ladybug and stepped back. "You're doing very well, Taylor. Just remember to keep those heels down and you should be fine."

"Got it," Taylor said. "Come on, Ladybug. Let's walk!"

The pony started walking as soon as

Taylor kicked her. She started to drift to the right again almost right away.

"No, you don't, naughty pony!" Taylor said with a laugh. She pulled firmly on the left rein. "We're going *this* way."

"Good job, Taylor!" Kara cried. "You're really riding!"

Taylor looked over and grinned. "I'm a cowboy!" she said. "Or wait, I mean a cow*girl*."

While she was talking, Ladybug drifted to the right again. A second later she was eating grass. Everyone laughed, and Ms. Sullivan stepped forward.

"I think Ladybug decided the ride is over," she joked. "But you did great, Taylor."

Emily bit her lip as Taylor jumped down and took off the riding helmet. Sure, Taylor had messed up a few times. But she'd hardly seemed to need Ms. Sullivan's advice at all! It didn't seem fair that she'd done so well when she didn't know much about ponies at all.

Maybe it's because she got to watch me and Kara go first, Emily thought. *Or maybe it's because she's so good at sports. She's used to learning stuff like this quickly.*

That made her feel a little better. Everyone knew that Taylor was great at anything athletic. At an earlier sleepover she'd learned to play croquet in about five minutes flat. And yesterday afternoon, she'd won every game of horseshoes. She seemed to be great at everything physical, from soccer to swimming. Why should riding be any different?

Next it was Jo's turn. She seemed a little nervous at first. She kept asking Ms. Sullivan if she was doing it right. But Ms. Sullivan always said yes. She didn't have to remind her about her reins or her heels once—not even when she trotted. And when Ms. Sullivan let her ride Ladybug on her own, Jo got the hungry pony to walk all the way around the yard without stopping to eat grass even once.

"That was terrific, Jo," Ms. Sullivan said when she finished. "You sit really well in the saddle. Are you sure you've never ridden before?"

"Only the pony rides at the fair," Jo said.

Ms. Sullivan smiled. "Well, you're a natural!"

Emily couldn't believe her ears. Jo, a natural at riding?

If anyone should be a natural, it should be me! she thought. *Jo isn't that interested in horses—she doesn't even have any pets!*

Suddenly the pony party didn't seem quite as much fun anymore. In fact, Emily felt a little like she might cry. She took a few deep breaths. She didn't want her friends to notice that anything was wrong.

"Time to go inside for a snack," Emily's

mother said as Jo got off the pony. "Let's give Ladybug a break."

"Aw, are you sure?" Taylor said. "She doesn't look tired."

Ms. Sullivan smiled. "Don't worry, girls," she said. "Go have your snack, and then we can try another ride when you're finished. I'll stay out here with Ladybug and let her eat some grass. That will be *her* snack."

Taylor, Kara, and Jo still looked a little disappointed as they walked inside. But Emily was secretly relieved. This pony party wasn't going the way she'd expected at all!

"That was so much fun, wasn't it?" Kara's eyes sparkled with excitement. "I mean, it was a little scary. But Ladybug is so cute!"

"I know." Jo glanced back at the pony as they walked inside. "I can't wait to try again."

Taylor skipped into the house. One of

Emily's stuffed horses was decorating the front hallway. Taylor gave it a pat as she passed.

"Who knew ponies were so much fun?" she said. "Ladybug is a lot cooler than the ponies at the fair, isn't she?"

Emily wasn't really listening. She was still thinking about their rides. She had spent almost her whole life learning everything she could about ponies and riding. So why wasn't she better at it? It didn't seem fair.

Kara elbowed her and giggled. "Check it out, guys," she said. "Em is so happy she forgot how to talk."

"Yeah," Taylor added. "She probably only speaks Pony now, not English."

The others laughed. Emily made herself smile, though she didn't really feel like smiling at all. Suddenly, seeing all the pony-themed decorations in the house was making her feel upset rather than happy. What was wrong with her?

She was quiet during their snack. Luckily, her friends didn't notice. They were too busy chattering about Ladybug.

When they went back outside, Mrs. McDougal brought an apple cut into several pieces. It was a treat for Ladybug. The pony was grazing in the yard, with Ms. Sullivan holding her lead rope.

"Let Emmers feed her the first piece," Taylor said.

Suddenly Emily couldn't stand it anymore. "Why don't you let Jo do it?" she blurted out before she could stop herself. "*She's* the natural!"

Then she burst into tears right in front of her surprised friends and raced back inside.

8

Lessons Learned

"Emily? Can I come in?"

Emily sat up and wiped her eyes. Her mother was standing in the doorway to her bedroom.

"Okay, I guess," Emily said with a sniffle.

Mrs. McDougal came in, sat down on the edge of the bed, and put her arm around her daughter. She looked concerned.

"What's wrong?" she asked. "Did you get scared of the pony?"

"No!" Emily shook her head. More tears started coming. "No, it's not that."

"What is it, then?" Now her mother looked confused.

Emily took a deep breath. She felt embarrassed. But she always told her mother the truth.

"I wish I was better at riding!" she admitted. "It's not fair that Jo and Taylor are better than me. They don't know anything about horses."

"I see." Mrs. McDougal sighed. "Oh, Emily. I can understand how you're feeling. But everyone learns different things at different speeds. There are things you're better at than most people, like school."

Emily frowned. "But I don't care about that," she said. "I want to be good at *riding*."

"Okay." Her mother squeezed her shoulder. "But all you can do is your best. You'll get there if you just keep trying and stay positive."

Emily sighed. How was she supposed to get better at riding if her parents thought she was too young for lessons? No, today was her only chance. And she'd messed it up.

She didn't say that to her mother, though. Her parents hated whining.

"Okay," she said instead. She took a deep breath. "Sorry for acting like such a baby."

"It's all right." Her mother rubbed her back and smiled. "Now, your friends are worried about you. Can they come in?"

Emily bit her lip. She felt stupid about getting so upset. But she nodded.

Soon Taylor, Jo, and Kara came rushing in. "Are you okay?" Kara cried, jumping on the bed and giving Emily a hug. "What's wrong?"

"Yeah, why were you so upset?" Taylor asked. "Did a bee sting you or something? That always makes me cry."

Jo was hanging back a little. She looked almost as upset as Emily felt.

"Are you mad at me, Emily?" she asked. "I don't know what I did, but I'm sorry."

That made Emily feel guilty. "I'm not

mad at you, Jo," she said. "I guess, um, I'm just a little bit jealous of you."

Jo's eyes widened. "What are you talking about?"

Emily told them the same thing she'd just told her mother. "All this time I figured I would be the one who was good at riding and taking care of ponies," she explained. "I'm the one who likes them and knows about them."

"That's right." Taylor nodded. "You've read more books about horses than anyone else I know, Emmers."

Emily felt tears welling up again. "But look at what happened," she said in a quivery voice. "I did worse than anyone except Kara! Sorry, Kara," she added.

"It's okay," Kara said.

Emily glanced over at her shelves full of horse books and model horses. "Maybe I should just give up on riding and ponies and everything."

"What?" Taylor looked horrified. "You can't do that! You love that stuff!"

"Taylor's right," Kara said, and Jo nodded.

"But what's the point?" Emily swung her legs against the edge of her bed. "I'm no good at it. I probably never will be."

"That's not true," Taylor insisted. "You can get better if you try hard enough. Just look at me. I used to think I'd *never* learn to swim!"

Emily blinked in surprise. "What are you talking about? You're a great swimmer."

"I am *now*," Taylor said. "But you should have seen me the first time I got in a pool." She giggled. "I sank!"

"Really?" Emily said.

"Uh-huh. But I kept taking lessons and practicing as hard as I could. And I got better and better."

Jo nodded. "That's how I was with

the clarinet," she said. "The first few months I took lessons, all I could do most of the time was squeak and squawk." She smiled. "Later on, after I got better, my dad told me it used to sound like two grumpy cats fighting every time I practiced."

"Wow." Emily was surprised by that, too. Jo took a clarinet lesson every week and played in the school band. She was really good.

"See, Em?" Kara hugged Emily again. "All you have to do is try, try again! So come outside and try again. Please? Ladybug misses you!"

Emily wiped her eyes one more time. She was still embarrassed about how she'd acted. But she nodded.

"Okay," she agreed. "Let's go."

When they got outside, Ms. Sullivan pretended nothing was wrong. She had Ladybug all ready to go.

"Who's first?" she asked cheerfully.

Emily glanced at her friends. "Maybe we should switch the order this time," she said. "That's only fair."

Her friends exchanged a worried look. But Jo nodded.

"Okay," she said. "I guess that means I'm first."

Emily watched as all three of her friends rode again. They all got to practice starting, stopping, and steering. Jo and Taylor even got to try trotting without Ms. Sullivan leading them. Kara didn't want to try that, but she did manage to hold the reins this time.

Then it was Emily's turn again. She took a deep breath and stepped forward.

"Here you go, Em," Kara said. She held out the riding helmet, which she had just taken off.

Emily reached for it. But just then her father stepped forward.

"Wait!" he said. "Before you ride, Emily, we have something for you."

Emily's mother stepped forward with a smile. She was holding a big, gift-wrapped box. "Here you go," she said. "Open it!"

9

A Dream Come True

Emily was confused. "What's this?" she said. "It's not my birthday or anything."

She looked over at her friends. They were all grinning at one another.

"Go on, open it, Emmers," Taylor urged.

Emily still had no idea what was going on. But she took the box from her mother. Even though it was big enough to hold one of Taylor's soccer balls, it felt very light. She set it down on the stump and unwrapped it.

Inside was a box with a picture of a riding helmet on it. When Emily opened the lid, a helmet was inside. It looked sort of like Ms. Sullivan's, only newer and shinier. Plus it was pink instead of black.

"Surprise!" Mrs. McDougal said. "We know how much you've always loved being around ponies and horses, Emily. We thought you were too young to get involved in that sort of thing before, but lately you've been growing up—just look at how responsible and mature you've been with planning these sleepovers, for instance!"

Hearing that made Emily feel a teensy bit ashamed. She certainly hadn't acted very mature by running off just now!

"Um, thanks," she said, looking down at the helmet. "I love it. It will look great on the horse shelf in my room."

Kara laughed. "Wait, she doesn't get it!" she cried.

"Yes, Felicity." Mr. McDougal chuckled and glanced at his wife. "You've confused her by talking too much, as usual."

"Huh?" Emily looked around at all of them, more confused than ever.

Mrs. McDougal poked Mr. McDougal in the shoulder. Then she smiled at Emily.

"This helmet is more than just a helmet," she said.

"Yeah," Kara cried out happily. "It means you're getting riding lessons!"

"Surprise, Emmers!" Taylor added, clapping her hands.

"Your parents told us about it just now while you were upstairs," Jo explained.

Emily gasped. "Really?" she exclaimed, hardly daring to believe it. "Riding lessons?"

"That's right, Emily." Ms. Sullivan stepped forward. "You'll be coming to my farm once a week and learning to ride Ladybug for real."

"Wow!" Emily took a step toward Ladybug, who was eating grass at the end of her lead rope. "Did you hear that, Ladybug?"

She walked over to give the pony a hug. Her head was spinning and she wasn't sure how to feel. This was what she had always wanted. But after finding out she wasn't as good a rider as she'd expected, did she still want it?

Behind her, she heard her friends chattering about this big news. That reminded her of the stories they had told her just a few minutes earlier.

When Taylor first tried to swim, she sank, Emily reminded herself. *When Jo tried to play the clarinet, she sounded horrible. But look at them now! Taylor swims like a fish, and Jo plays beautiful music. That's because they took lessons and practiced. Maybe the same thing will work for me!*

She remembered all her daydreams about galloping off on a magical horse like the unicorn in that movie. Riding a real live pony had turned out to be very different from that. But maybe if she worked hard, she could make those dreams come true someday.

Ladybug was snuffling at her hair by now. Emily gave her one last hug, then turned away. She hurried over to her parents.

"Thank you so much!" she said, giving them each a big hug. She turned and smiled at Ms. Sullivan. "I can't wait to become a real rider!"

"Okay, then let's start right now." Ms. Sullivan led Ladybug toward the stump. "Put on that new helmet and climb up!"

The new helmet felt great. Being in the saddle again felt good too. This time Emily mounted correctly on her first try. She kept her heels down almost the entire time. And at the end of her turn she even got

Ladybug to trot halfway across the yard—
all by herself! That felt *really* great!

"Terrific job, Emily!" Ms. Sullivan said
when she stopped. "See? You're learning
already."

"Ride 'em, cowgirl!" Taylor cheered.

Emily grinned, feeling happy and excited
and proud of herself. "Giddyup, Ladybug!"
she cheered back.

Slumber Party Project:
What's Your Theme?

The next time you plan a sleepover with your friends, why not make it a theme party? Emily's sleepover had a pony theme. But you can invent any theme you want—part of the fun is coming up with great ideas for food, games, and decorations to match the theme. Here's one example:

Hooray for Hollywood! Pretend you and your friends are big stars at a Hollywood party. For decorations, cut out shiny gold or silver stars and write your names on them. Make star-shaped cookies. Get dressed up like movie stars, lay down a "red carpet," and take pictures of one another. After that—what else? Stay up late watching all your favorite movies!

Get the idea? Then here are a few more theme ideas to get you started. Throw one of these parties, or come up with your own great idea for a theme. Have fun!

Calling All Princesses!
(Fantasy fun theme; unicorns, fairies, and more!)

Out of This World!
(Outer space theme)

Jungle Fun
(Animals, animals, animals!)

Beach Party
(No *real* beach required!)

YOU'RE INVITED TO A SLEEPOVER!

Join the Sleepover Squad for
their first four sleepovers!

Sleeping Over

Camping Out

The Trouble
With Brothers

Keeping Secrets